My Lucky Day

Keiko Kasza

SCHOLASTIC INC.

New York Toronto London Auckland Sydney
Mexico City New Delhi Hong Kong Buenos Aires

For Hiroki

ISBN 0-439-67324-0

30 29 28 27   18 19 20/0

Printed in the U.S.A.   40

First Scholastic printing, November 2004

Designed by Gunta Alexander
Text set in Administer.
The art was done in gouache on three-ply Bristol illustration paper.

One day, a hungry fox was preparing to hunt for his dinner. As he polished his claws, he was startled by a knock at the door.

"Hey, Rabbit!" someone yelled outside. "Are you home?"

Rabbit? thought the fox. *If there were any rabbits in here, I'd have eaten them for breakfast.*

When the fox opened the door, there stood a delicious-looking piglet.

"Oh, no!" screamed the piglet.

"Oh, yes!" cried the fox. "You've come to the right place."

He grabbed the piglet and hauled him inside.

"This must be my lucky day!" the fox shouted. "How often does dinner come knocking on the door?"

The piglet kicked and squealed, "Let me go! Let me go!"

"Sorry, pal," said the fox. "This isn't just any dinner. It's a pig roast. My favorite! Now get into this roasting pan."

It was useless to struggle. "All right," sighed the
piglet. "I will. But there is just one thing."

"What?" growled the fox.

"Well, I am a pig, you know. I'm filthy. Shouldn't
you wash me first? Just a thought, Mr. Fox."

"Hmmm . . ." the fox said to himself, "he is filthy."

So the fox got busy.

He collected twigs.

He made a fire.

He carried in the water.

And, finally, he gave the piglet a nice bath.
"You're a terrific scrubber," said the piglet.

"There," said the fox. "Now you're the cleanest piglet in the county. You stay still, now!"

"All right," sighed the piglet. "I will. But . . ."

"But what?" growled the fox.

"Well, I am a very small piglet, you know. Shouldn't you fatten me up to get more meat? Just a thought, Mr. Fox."

"Hmmm . . ." the fox said to himself, "he is on the small side."

So the fox got busy.

He picked tomatoes.

He made spaghetti.

He baked cookies.

And, finally, he gave the piglet a nice dinner.
"You're a terrific cook," said the piglet.

"There," said the fox. "Now you're the fattest piglet in the county. So get into the oven!"

"All right," sighed the piglet. "I will. But . . ."

"What? What? WHAT?" shouted the fox.

"Well, I am a hardworking pig, you know. My meat is awfully tough. Shouldn't you massage me first to make a more tender roast? Just a thought, Mr. Fox."

"Hmmm . . ." the fox said to himself, "I do prefer tender meat."

So the fox got busy.

He pushed . . .

and he pulled.

He squeezed and he pounded the piglet from head to toe.
"You give a terrific massage," said the piglet.

"But," the piglet continued, "I've been working really hard lately. My back is awfully stiff. Could you push a bit harder, Mr. Fox? A little to the right, please . . . yes, yes . . . now just a little to the left . . .

"Mr. Fox, are you there?"

But Mr. Fox was no longer listening. He had passed out, exhausted. He couldn't lift a finger, let alone a roasting pan.

"Poor Mr. Fox," sighed the piglet. "He's had a busy day." Then the cleanest, fattest and softest piglet in the county picked up the rest of his cookies and headed for home.

"What a bath! What a dinner! What a massage!"
cried the piglet. "This must be my lucky day!"

When he got home, the piglet relaxed before a warm fire. "Let's see," he wondered, looking at his address book. "Who shall I visit next?"

Fox
Log Cabin
up on the hill

Wolf
Next to the
tallest pine
tree

Bear
House with
red roof by
the river

Coyote
Cave under
the hanging
rock